Wake Up Desmond

Rowena Portch
&
Sheryl Anne Sanchez Lugtu

Ukiyoto Publishing

All global publishing rights are held by

Ukiyoto Publishing

Published in 2020

Content Copyright ©

Rowena Portch & Sheryl Anne Sanchez Lugtu

Cover Art by Rowena Portch

ISBN 9789364946735

*All rights reserved.
No part of this publication may be reproduced, transmitted, or stored in a retrieval system, in any form by any means, electronic, mechanical, photocopying, recording or otherwise, without the prior permission of the publisher.*

The moral rights of the author have been asserted.

This is a work of fiction. Names, characters, businesses, places, events, locales, and incidents are either the products of the author's imagination or used in a fictitious manner. Any resemblance to actual persons, living or dead, or actual events is purely coincidental.

This book is sold subject to the condition that it shall not by way of trade or otherwise, be lent, resold, hired out or otherwise circulated, without the publisher's prior consent, in any form of binding or cover other than that in which it is published.

Dedication from Sheryl

To Aurora and Evelyn,

whose love is eternal

Acknowledgement

First, I would like to thank God, Most Holy, for his guidance as we write this story. When we were beginning, these are all a blank slate but through his blessings of wisdom and knowledge, we were able to pull this through.

Thank you to my family: The Tanguanco Family. To Tito Ed, Tita Butch, Tito Alvin, Tita Chu, Anika, Tito Rainier... to Ate Lits and Ate Yhane for all the love and support.

To Rowena, who has been so kind and supportive throughout the whole process and Gregg who made our story look great.

To Zeke, who drew me closer to God and inspires me to write more. To Lennard, Ays, and JL for being my supportive bestfriends all the time.

And to all of you who believed in me, thank you!

-Anne

Every journey begins with a step. Mine began with curiosity; an adventure that would forever change my life.

My mother had ordered me to stay in the car while she finished grocery shopping, but I was captivated by a red object floating in the sky! What was it? What kept it in the air? We had just returned from the doctor's office. I had been blind since birth and had undergone my second eye-replacement operation. He said my eyes were healing well and that it would take time for me to figure things out.

The red object fluttered in the air, dancing like a fat cloud. Then, it floated behind a tree. Not wanting to lose sight of the magical orb, I got out of the car and ran to where I thought it had flown. There it was, pushing its way between streets. *Was it really that fast?* I wondered. I continued to run, enjoying the freedom to do so, because I no longer needed a white cane to detect obstructions. I could see them, even though I had little idea of what I was seeing. The challenge was determining how far away things really were. They looked much closer yet I could not touch them. This magical red flying orb was so magnificent that I reached out several times to touch it, but never could.

I ran into an older woman who shouted, "Hey there. Watch where you're going!"

Pointing to the sky, I asked, "What is that?"

She looked at me, her face skewed between thick white brows, her lips arched downward. "It's just a balloon."

"A balloon?" My mind flashed back as I remembered touching one on my fifth birthday. It was soft and squishy and had a sharp scent, like burnt meat. That one never flew, though. It just dropped to the floor when I released it. This one was special. "Thank you," I shouted over my shoulder before continuing to run after it, hoping it would eventually fall back to down so I could find out how it flew. It had to fall, right? I had been told that airplanes and birds could stay in the air, but I'd never heard about balloons being able to fly.

It disappeared over the hills, so I continued to run, struggling to catch my breath. My muscles ached and my heart pounded so loud, I was certain it would break through my ribs. My legs quivered and collapsed beneath me. My head felt funny and my vision blurred a bit. What was happening to me?

Someone approached me. "Hey, are you okay?" It was an older man with a raspy voice. "What are ya doin' out here, boy?" His rough hands gripped my arm and hauled me to my feet.

"The balloon," I huffed, pointing to the tallest peak of the hills. "It fell over there."

The old man huffed. "Well, it's gone now. Ya best return back home."

I looked around at hill after hill of golden grass. Nothing seemed familiar. "Can you tell me how to get back to the grocery store?"

The old man's face wrinkled. "Which grocery store, son? There are several of them in town."

I had not learned how to read letters yet, nor did I know what color they were. "Um, it's the one with a café in the front, and a deli on the right." The scent of them flooded my memory like old friends offering comfort.

He huffed, and then rattled off the names of the surrounding stores, but all of them sounded familiar. Which one had my mother chosen today?

"I'm n—not sure." Mill Valley was a small city compared to the neighboring icon of San Francisco. It seemed much smaller when I was blind; everything was smaller. Now that I could see, I felt like a microbe under a microscope, living in the vastness of so much space. The world was much larger than I had ever imagined. It went far beyond what I could smell, touch, hear, and feel, which is probably why Mom told me to stay in the car. For two years, the world seemed to revolve around my house and yard. I wasn't even allowed to watch the television because the radiation may have affected my eyes. I became easily disoriented in public places; something my doctor promised would fade with time. He said that I might've been getting used to my vision.

The old man continued, "You don't look so good, son. Come back to the house with me and I'll get you some water."

"I'm just a bit winded is all. I'm not used to running." I said while catching my breath.

He snorted. "You're a pint under teenage. I take it you don't play sports. Youngins these days do little more than play video games on those gosh darn devices they call phones. I'm assuming you're one of 'em?" He glanced back at me, as if I were a worm too small to fish with.

Expressions were new to me, but his, all scrunched up and a bit scary, did not leave me with a good feeling. I followed him down the path to a small cottage; or at least it looked like something I had read about in books. The log walls were much smoother than I had imagined and the inside smelled like simmering meat and sweet potatoes.

The old man gestured to a hard wooden chair at a table. "Have a seat."

A woman stepped around the corner wiping her hands with a towel that hung around her neck. She smelled like roses. Her trembling hand reached toward me.

"I'm Netta."

I gripped her delicate hand and shook it up and down as my dad had shown me. Her skin felt like paper, the kind my mom used to clean up messes.

Netta chuckled. "That's quite a grip you have, young man." She pulled her hand away and rubbed it with the other.

The old man set a cup of cold water in front of me. "Drink that down, and then I will drive you back to town."

Netta disappeared into another room and returned with two cookies. "There ya go, dear. You look like you can use a couple of treats."

"What's your name, kiddo?" asked the old man.

"I'm Desmond," I answered. "Desmond Shirk and I'm 12 years old." I remembered what mom told me. She said that I always have to include my age whenever people are asking. I dunno why, though.

The old man reached out his weathered hand. "I'm Joe."

Netta smiled, but the emotion didn't reach her eyes. "What a nice name you have there. If our Luke was still here, he would be very glad to have you as company." Her eyes glistened and a rush of emotions poured out.

I chomped the cookie. It was crispy, just the way I liked it, and it had raisins and chocolate chips. I eagerly took another bite, thinking about what the old woman said. Was Luke their son? Half way through my second cookie, I asked the old woman, "Who was Luke?"

Her grey eyes stared out the window, glistened with tears. She sniffed. "He was our son, dear. Died of Pneumonia one winter." She wiped her eyes and stood from her chair. "No matter. It happened long ago."

Not knowing what to say, I finished my treat in silence and downed the water that tasted like dusty copper. I thought about Mom and how worried she would be when she discovered I was gone. "I should probably get back to the store now." I stood and carried my plate and cup to the sink. "Thank you for the sweets and water."

Netta smiled down at me. She wasn't much taller than I was. "You're a good boy." She patted my head.

The old man entered the room. "Got the old Chevy running. Are you ready to go?"

I nodded, and then shook Netta's hand. "It was nice to meet you." This time, I didn't squeeze so hard.

"You too, dear," she chuckled.

The old truck idled roughly as we approached it almost acting like it did not approve of us taking the trip. The door squeaked as I opened it and I could smell the rust on the hinges. It was a struggle climbing into the large cab, but I managed to settle into the cracked vinyl seat and fasten the seat belt. Mom said the car would not move unless everyone secured their safety belts. I'm not sure if the same were true for old trucks. Mold, dust, and decaying foam assaulted my nose. It reminded me of an old movie theater my father took me to. I couldn't see the movie, but spending time with my dad and eating popcorn while he described the action to me was worth every minute. I looked forward to repeating the outing now that I had new eyes.

We entered the parking lot of Trader Joe's but my mother's car was not where we left it.

Joe huffed, his mouth turned downward. "Are you sure this is the right store?" I was beginning to wonder if this was his normal expression. Was he always grumpy? I remember, after my surgery, my father showed me what expressions looked like. They made me laugh as he mimicked happiness, pride, and sadness. But, when he made an angry face, it looked a lot like this old man's.

Glancing around the parking lot, I said, "Yes, I'm sure."

"Do you live far from here?"

My parents made sure that my siblings and I remembered our address. I had to repeat it over and over like some sacred mantra until Mom was certain I would never forget it. "21 Somerset Lane."

Joe grumbled. "I don't know where that is."

I had heard Dad give directions to people and repeated them now. "Highway 101, Blithedale Ave exit."

"Blithedale? That's clear across town. I best take you to the Central Marin Police Authority. That is where your mother will be."

We drove a few miles and pulled up to a brick building with a dark green metal roof. The place reminded me of the administration building at school.

"Wait here." I watched as Joe stepped from the cab and slammed the rusty door. "What's your mom's name again?" he asked.

"Aurora Shirk," I called out the window.

He nodded to another man as he passed and entered the building. I looked around the parking lot for my mother's car but didn't see it. A sick feeling tickled my belly as Joe returned to the truck.

Without saying a word, he turned the key and revved the engine.

"Joe? What's going on?"

"She wasn't there. I gave the police my information and told them I was taking you to my home. If your mother files a missing person's report, they will know where to find you."

I didn't want to go back with him. My mother would not have just left without me, I know it. "I may have gotten the store wrong. Can we check the others in town?"

The corners of Joe's mouth dropped further, as if the muscles that held them gave up. "It's gettin' late, son. We best get home now."

The thought of staying at a stranger's house frightened me, but the sun was beginning to set and it would be dark and cold soon. I had nowhere else to go. I wished I had my iPhone, but I had left it in Mom's car. Her number was programmed into my contact list and all I had to do was ask Siri to call Mom. I didn't remember her phone number, or my dad's.

Joe glanced down at my lap. "Stop wringing your hands, boy, or your skin will fall off."

"I need to contact my mom and dad. They will be worried about me."

"Then you shouldn't have run off!" His angry retort sent a shiver down my spine. I stared out the window at the rolling hillside, my mind racing with options and horrid scenarios. Was I in danger?

I had no idea that balloon had taken me so far. It seemed to take forever to drive back to Joe and Netta's place. As we meandered our way up the long and curvy drive, Netta stood on the front porch with a confused look on her face.

My father would have described this house as a rambler with a wrap-around porch. Painted in dark brown with green trim, it blended with the surrounding hills as if it had grown here. What would ever possess two people to live this far from town?

When Joe made it clear that I was spending the night, Netta's face lit up like a Christmas Santa displayed in a yard. She fed me stew, fresh bread, and peach pie for dessert. They had an old computer. I thought I could access my contact list through the internet, but without my screen-reading software, I didn't know how to navigate.

Joe stood beside Netta and me as she tried to help me. Joe humphed. "I thought all kids your age knew how to work these things."

"I have only used them with JAWS."

Both Joe and Netta looked at me as if I had sprung wings out of my back or something equally weird.

Joe's face scrunched up. "Like the movie?"

"It's a screen-reading software for blind people."

Netta studied my eyes as if looking for clues to an intriguing mystery. "You're not blind."

"Not anymore," I explained. "I was born blind. My doctor gave me new eyes two years ago, but having sight is still new to me since I wasn't allowed to go out 'til I finished all my therapies."

Netta's brows wrinkled. "But, why did it take so long? Usually those who had their eyes operated on could recover within months or a year at the most."

"Well, the first operation was a mess, and resulted in the most pain I have felt in my life. My eyes would sometimes bleed. So, they did another operation last year. Fortunately, I recovered faster." I remembered how Mom and Dad struggled just to pay for the procedure. They both work two jobs to settle the bills. They even had to get a loan because the second operation wasn't covered by our health insurance.

My thoughts drifted to my mom. She must be frantic with worry. Dad probably left work to be with her. I wrung my hands, feeling helpless and frustrated.

Netta must have sensed my despair. She drew herself closer and touched my head. "Don' t worry, my son. Everything will be alright. We will be in-charge of you for now." Her eyes glistened. Within those brilliant blue-grey irises, I sensed her genuine concern and compassion toward me.

Forcing a smile, I said, "Thank you, ma'am. I appreciate it."

She patted my back and said, "Okay, then. I'll show you to your room. Follow me."

Joe went back outside, grumbling something under his breath. I looked after him as the front door slammed behind him.

Netta waved her wrinkled hand at the door. "Never mind Joe. He's been in a fit ever since our goats have been kidding. He hasn't slept much over the past few nights.

I didn't remember seeing goats anywhere. "You have goats?"

"Many. We make our living selling milk, cheese, and soap to the local markets." She led me down a long hallway with three closed doors. She tapped the second door on the right. "This is your bathroom." She continued to the next door on the left and opened it. "And this is your bedroom." She rushed over and stripped the bed of Spiderman sheets and covers. "I'll fetch you fresh linen." Her hands shook as she carried the bedding out of the room.

Posters of race cars and Nascar drivers covered the walls. There were a few pictures of Marvel characters, mingled with a variety of framed baseball cards, Star Wars posters, and soccer trophies. A huge dresser took up most of the wall under the window. Across from that were shelves of books. I couldn't read but most of them looked like they had been enjoyed multiple times. The pages were crumpled and turned down at some of the corners. The spines were loose as if they had been broken over and over again.

Netta returned with fresh bedding. I helped her make the bed, noticing the stiffness of her movements. Her lips were tight and straight, her eyes unfocused.

"Are you okay, Netta?"

She smiled, but it never reached her eyes. "I'm fine, dear." She snapped a pillow case open and forced the fluffy pillow inside as if she were wrestling a cat during bath time. "I'll leave you be now, so you can rest." She gestured for me to get into bed, and then tucked me in. With gnarled fingers and a saddened expression, she closed the lights and left the room.

I tried to close my eyes and force myself to sleep but the darkness just made me reminisce about happy moments with my family. Suddenly, there was a loud thud. My eyes opened wide. I felt a chill on my spine. I couldn't understand why the darkness, which used to be my solace, scared me so much now. Next came a crash... I wondered what it was so I stood and listened through the door. All I heard was a lot of mumbling. Quietly opening the door, I walked past the bathroom and padded into the kitchen. I could hear Netta murmuring something but could not make out the words.

I moved closer to their bedroom, feeling sneaky and wrong. I heard Netta speak more harshly than I ever thought possible from her. "I can't believe you lied to me, Joe. How could you?"

Joe cleared his throat. "Calm down now dear. I was just trying to make you happy again. The smile you had when you saw the boy was something I haven't witnessed in a while. I wanted to give you hope."

"Hope," she barked. "My God, Joe, have you any idea how hard this is for me? How hard this must be for Desmond?"

"I just wanted to keep him for a little while." Another crash followed that statement as if something had been tossed against the wall.

I crept backward, not wanting to be noticed. Hurrying back to my room, I quietly closed the door. So, Joe never did report my whereabouts to the police. The betrayal felt bitter and rancid in my stomach. Joe had looked me straight in the eyes when he lied. Memories of when my younger sister Maex had given me a gift for my birthday three years ago flooded my mind and fueled my disgust. She said it was a box of M&Ms. I opened it, excited to enjoy the rare treat. The box did not contain candy, it harbored a horde of spiders that crawled all over my hand and arms, digging their fangs into my flesh as I frantically brushed them off.

Maex laughed at me, enjoying my pain and fear. She may not have understood it at that time because she was too young, but I felt like a fool and she relished it. The pain of being tricked felt worse than the spiders' bites, even though they made me sick for days after.

I looked outside the window and noticed the dark clouds covering the sky. Leaving now was not a good idea. I would have to wait for early morning. I didn't trust Joe anymore and didn't want him to drive me anywhere. I had to make it back to town and find someone to help me get home.

I was awakened by the sweet smell of baked bananas and cinnamon. *Muffins,* I thought. I couldn't be wrong. Muffins were a huge part of my childhood. Granny Evelyn, or Granny Eve as I call her, would always cook muffins for everyone. I spent most of my happy memories with her. She would bring me to an orphanage where she would always deliver her muffins. I met all of the children and I could feel how happy they were even if I could not see the smiles on their faces. Too bad, she died of Leukemia when I was 8 years old. I missed her sweet disposition and her baking.

I stood and arranged the sheets, thinking of my plan. As I looked out the window, I saw Joe outside, tending to his goats. I hadn't expected him to be up so early. My family barely started moving before eight o'clock. It must be close to six now and Netta was making muffins while Joe was out and about. Now what?

The ground was only six feet down from the window, but I would have to wait for Joe to be out of sight or he would certainly see me. Joe fired up the tractor. Now was the perfect time to open the window and remove the screen, something my father made seem easy. These windows were very different from the ones at home.

There was an odd, circular contraption on the top that kept the window closed. I turned it counter-clockwise and the window made a popping sound. I cringed, hoping Netta hadn't heard it. I lifted the wood frame expecting it to be heavy, yet it slid up easily, as two heavy objects rattled behind the window frame. Intrigued, I noticed the pulleys at the top of the inside frame. I moved the window up and down, and heard what must have been counterweights. How cool.

A sharp sound came from the kitchen as Netta dropped a pan. The crash jolted me back to purpose and I returned to the task at hand. The window screens at home were much different than this old thing. Ours had a tag that we used to pull up the screen so it could be removed. Since cleaning the windows and screens were one of my chores, I became very proficient at it. This screen had no such tag and looked to be seated solidly in the frame.

"Desmond?" I heard Netta say as her footsteps grew louder. My heart raced. There was no time to open the screen, so I dove onto the bed and pulled up the covers.

The door creaked open. "Desmond?" Netta approached the bed, pulling the covers up over my shoulders. I stopped breathing, not wanting her to see the rise and fall of my rapid breath. "Poor child. Sleep now. I'll save breakfast for you." She patted my arm and left the room. I waited until the door clicked shut before stirring. My sister and I had perfected this technique as we were nearly caught reading scary stories when we were supposed to be sleeping.

I heard Netta set the table and Joe's tractor turn off. He would be coming in for breakfast soon. I hadn't much time. My dad always said I was mechanically inclined, which I later learned meant I could easily figure out how things worked. That particular mojo was needed now. I felt around the screen's frame, looking for something that offered any clue on how to remove it. Odd how I still relied more on my sense of touch over the use of my sight. My doctor said it was normal to return to what was familiar. He said in time, my sight would eventually take over my other senses. I seriously doubted it.

Having sight was cool, but my other senses provided information that my sight still lacked.

Two indentations on the bottom of the screen frame housed spring-loaded mechanisms. I pushed them inward and the screen swung away but not free. I could slip through well enough, so I did, though my landing was less than graceful. If it were not for the pile of leaves, the ground would have been much harder. Joe was nowhere in sight, so I trotted off toward the back where I would not be seen.

At the end of the driveway, I turned left and headed toward town, happy that I had paid enough attention to the roads Joe had taken to the police station. It would be a long walk and my stomach continued to remind me that I had yet to feed it breakfast. Remembering the sweet scent of those muffins made my stomach ache all the more.

It felt good to be out in the morning sun. Oddly enough, the brightness of it didn't hurt my eyes like it used to. Before the surgery, any light at all felt like a red-hot poker in my brain. I was told to wear dark glasses when I was outside until my new eyes had a chance to adapt. Like my phone, I left my shades in the car when I chased that darn balloon.

I smiled inwardly, relishing my new-found freedom. I felt like Tom Sawyer on one of his adventures. Mom and Dad had been so protective of me, I was not allowed to do anything, it seemed. The doctors, too, were overly cautious. My first surgery was such a disaster, it had everyone on high alert. I guess I should be just as concerned, but caution was at the back of the line compared to the way I felt this moment.

The pavement crunched under my feet with each step. Everything seemed dull and quiet since my vision had been restored. For a moment, I closed my eyes and eased into the comfort of using my other senses. I inhaled the sweet smell of morning dew and it calmed me down a bit. Without the aid of my white cane, walking with my eyes closed was a challenge, but not scary or impossible. The cliffs echoed the sound of my steps. The narrow back road had no traffic as I continued along, feeling the warmth of the sun on my face. When the side of my foot felt the soft edge of the shoulder, I adjusted my direction as easily as if I had seen the curve of the road. It felt natural and familiar.

Shadows covered the road, causing me to open my eyes. Gigantic trees lined a path that looked too inviting to ignore. I veered off the main road and chose to explore this new one made of red dirt. I was stunned by the beauty that lay before me. Leaves shone as the rays of sunlight creeped past through them. This would be a long journey, but I knew I would eventually reach my destination. Instinctively curious, I reached out to touch the rough bark of a tree. The trunk was so large, my arms could not reach around to even a quarter of its diameter. Memories of when my father took me to the Redwood forest near Crescent City flooded my mind. I remembered touching the large timbers, but I had never imagined them to be this massive. Yes, they were thick in girth, but these were so tall, I could barely see their tops. The scent of the bark stung my nose with its strong acidic oils.

On the ground around them grew shamrock-looking plants. I bent down to touch them. They felt familiar, like the plants my father had me try once. They tasted very lemony and tart. Carefully, I plucked a three-leafed clover from its stem and placed it in my mouth. Dad called them Mountain Sorrel. They were delicate and left my mouth feeling refreshed. Dad had warned me not to eat too many or they could make me sick. I continued on my way, reveling in being able to see what I had only experienced as a blind person. Things looked much different than I had imagined. Then again, I did not have any memories of vision to base my imagination on, so my mind created maps based on input from my other senses. They were similar to 3-D grids of sorts, like what a computer design program generated, only not as sophisticated.

While I was walking, an animal crossed the road. I was not familiar with it though it had the shiniest eyes I had ever seen. It looked at me as if it were trying to tell me something. Its tail was fluffy, sporting a striking white stripe over its black pelt. It stopped for a moment, as if it were studying me. Seemingly satisfied with the assessment, it scurried into the woods. I wondered if he was lost too? Tears welled in my eyes as I suddenly missed my family and the familiarity of home. I wiped away the tears and continued walking. It would do no good to feel discouraged now. I had embarked on a journey and I had to see it through. This adventure might be new to me but I knew in my heart that at some point, I would find my way home again.

My stomach growled. It seemed I had been walking for hours and this path just continued on and on. Was there no end to it? I looked up at the bright streams of sunlight directly overhead now. It must be close to noon, I figured. No wonder I was so hungry. I heard a car speed past up ahead, indicating I was close to a road. My pace quickened and my hopes began to rise once again.

As expected, I reached the asphalt and decided to turn right. I heard a car approach from behind, so I scooted further onto the shoulder. The car slowly passed, and then turned onto the shoulder.

"Ya need a ride?" A man shouted.

I ran to the passenger door. The man was alone and had lowered the window. A faint scent of spearmint air freshener assaulted my nose. "Can you take me to the police station?"

The man smiled. "Sure, kid, get in. I'm going right past it."

I opened the door, remembering my mom warning us kids about accepting rides from strangers. If she found out what I was doing, she would be mad as a wet cat. The car was old, but comfortable.

"What's your name, kid?" His breath carried the scent of tobacco, which explained the large lump nestled beneath his lower lip. My uncle chewed tobacco. I never saw the draw for the disgusting habit.

"Desmond Shirk."

The man reached over with his right hand extended. "Ray Charles."

My eyes widened. I shook his hand with awe. "Like the singer?"

He laughed, and then spit into a container. "Same name, but not related." Having noticed my confusion and slight disappointment, he asked, "What are ya doin' all the way out here on your own?"

I sighed and my stomach rebelled with an audible grumble. "Long story."

Ray looked down at my rude belly. "Ya sounds hungry."

I shrugged. "Haven't had breakfast yet."

"How 'bout I buy ya something on our way into town? Ya like McDonald's?"

I perked up. Eating at McDonald's was a rare treat. Mom and Dad despised the place. "Sure!" Okay, not only was I riding in a car with a complete stranger, now I was accepting food from him? Mom would be in fits over this. Having been the kind of kid who always did the right thing, this felt wrong, but intriguing at the same time. I wondered if this is what it felt like to be an adult who could do anything they wanted—pretty much.

Ray pulled into the drive-through and asked me what I wanted.

Unable to read the menu, I went with something I remembered having with my family once. "Pancakes and hash browns, please."

Ray placed our order and then looked back to me. "Something to drink?"

I didn't have to think too hard about that one. "A chocolate shake."

The dark brows over Ray's eyes arched. "For breakfast?" Shaking his head, he finished our order and pulled forward to pay. He sort of reminded me of my uncle Steve; the fun one in the family. I had remembered how he took care of my sister and I one weekend. He fed us cake for breakfast, and ice cream for lunch. It was one of the best weekends ever. Ray was also lanky like uncle Steve—probably accentuated by his frumpy overalls that looked as if they had lost a battle with white paint.

Ray accepted the bags from a lady and handed them to me, along with my shake. He held his coffee as we pulled forward into a parking space. "I'm not so good at eating and driving, so we will eat here before we go, okay?"

I nodded, eagerly punching the straw into the lid of my chocolate shake. I took a long draw of the creamy treat and smiled. Another gulp quickly followed. My stomach growled with approval.

Ray divvied out the food, but before he could offer me the plastic utensils, I opened the cardboard box and folded a pancake into my mouth. They were much smaller than I had remembered, and there were only three of them. He was about to offer me syrup and salt, then hesitated as I ate the tiny hash brown cake. I hadn't remembered being this hungry. There might be times when we ran out of money but our dining table was never empty.

"Whoa ... slow down, Kiddo, before you choke." Ray chuckled.

I laughed as well, feeling far more comfortable with this stranger than I should have.

Mom would kill me for doing so but she wouldn't blame me. Ray was a very likable man.

He finished his meal and stuffed the container back into its bag. "When I saw you earlier, I thought you were just wanderin' around. Ya know, like kids your age. Never would've thought you were lost? Were you mesmerized by the view? Haven't ya been there before?"

I shook my head. "Nah. It was my first time." I chomped the last piece of hash brown and swallowed it down as if it were the last one I would ever enjoy.

"The station's only three blocks away from here. Your parents would have filed a missing persons report by now. I'm sure you'll be home by nightfall." His tobacco-stained teeth displayed a disgusting smile. He started the engine and headed down the highway.

The police station was a familiar and hopeful sight. As Ray parked the car, his phone rang. His eyebrows pinched together as he listened. "Hang on," he said to the other party. "Sorry, Kiddo. I gotta run. Will you be okay?"

I opened the door and smiled at him. "Yes, sir. Thank you for breakfast."

As I slammed the door shut, he opened the window. "You take care now, kid. I hope you find your family."

"I will. Thanks again."

Mill Valley Police Station was bustling with people. The contrasting scent of sweat and disinfectant made the food I had eaten far too quickly, churn in my stomach. Determined, I marched to the counter and asked to speak to an officer. The noise of constant chatter and angry conversations made my ears ring.

The woman at the counter slid a clipboard toward me and a pen. "Sign in, please. We'll call your name when we're ready."

I never had to sign my name before, and wasn't really sure how to do it. The other signatures on the page looked like scribble marks, so I drew a few wavy lines and pushed the clipboard back to the woman.

She took it with a bored expression. "Have a seat." She gestured to the crowded room of rowdy people.

I pointed outside. "Can I wait out there?"

The woman waved me off as if I were a nagging fly.

Eager to leave the chaos, I went outside. A woman was standing by the door, talking to a man who looked to be in his thirties.

"I'm pressing charges, Dave. You know what those animals are worth."

The man shook his head with disbelief. "Tori, I didn't steal them! I swear it."

I stood close to the man; close enough to where I could catch his scent. He wasn't lying, I knew it. People emitted a sharp vinegar-like aroma when they lied. This man smelled more like clove and synthetic pine cologne.

The woman pushed passed him toward the double-doors. "We'll let the courts decide."

I touched her arm as she strode past. The woman looked at me like a lion who just spotted its next meal.

"He's telling the truth." My words came out more like a choke.

Her eyes narrowed. "Excuse me?"

I pointed to the Hispanic man she had been talking to. "Your man, Dave, he's telling the truth."

She huffed and entered the station. I looked over at Dave who looked forlorn and confused.

"Thanks, kid," he said before walking away.

I sat on the cold stone bench as people entered and exited the building. I considered going back in to check my place in the queue, but after looking at the crowded lobby I changed my mind. I remembered a time when my mother and I were at the post office, waiting to mail a package. The room became so crowded that I had lost track of her. I was suddenly in the midst of strangers who were bumping into me. I called for my mom, but she never responded. The fear of that day prevented me from entering crowded spaces. My mom eventually found me, but she had to give up her space in line. She kept apologizing as if it was her fault that I was lost. I was the one who wandered off in search of her. If I had stayed put, she would have found me much quicker.

Memories of the red balloon that beckoned me so far from my mother's car flooded my mind like fresh fodder for guilt. Was she angry with me? Worried? She never could eat when she worried. My sister probably enjoyed me being gone. Now she would get all the attention. My heart ached with loneliness and regret. Judging by the angle of the sun, it was late afternoon. Dad would be heading home from work, and Mom would be cooking dinner. Maex was probably getting her homework done, or pretending to do so. I missed them all. I missed having dinner at the table and talking about our day. I missed having a hot bath, ice cream for dessert, and the hot cocoa Mom made just before bedtime. My chest felt as if it were being crushed by a trash compactor. I wanted to go home.

It seemed as if I had been waiting for a very long time. The sun continued its descent, nearly disappearing behind the hills. People began filing out of the building, grumbling as if they were angry. The woman named Tori came out as well and looked over at me. She stopped, and then approached.

"Hey, are you waiting for someone?"

I gestured toward the building. "I'm waiting for them to call my name."

She followed my stare and then looked back at me with sorrow—or was that pity? "Honey, they are closing now. What's your name?"

Again, I had been lied to. The woman said she would call my name. I was sitting out here this whole time for nothing. "Desmond."

Tori shook her head. "I have been in there the whole time and never heard them call that name. Can I give you a ride somewhere?"

"You wouldn't happen to be heading toward Mill Valley, would you?"

Her mouth twisted into a crooked grin. "No, I'm heading the opposite direction." She looked up at the darkening sky. "It's getting late. Why don't you come back with me and we can see about getting you a ride into town tomorrow morning?"

I stood, grimacing at the tingling burn down my legs. My feet had grown numb, so it took me a bit to get moving. Tori pointed toward a blue-gray sedan. "That's my car." She pressed a button on her keychain and the doors beeped twice. I opened the passenger door, marveling at the nice interior. I had never been in a car this fancy before. It had a shiny wood dash, and grey seats that were soft as velvet. My hand brushed against them.

Tori observed me and smiled. "Nice leather, right?"

Embarrassed, I fastened my seatbelt and placed my hands in my lap. She must think I'm a simpleton for being so fascinated with a car seat. "What kind of car is this?"

She pressed a button on the dash and the car sparked to life. The engine was so quiet, I could barely hear it. "Tesla. It's an electric car."

We rolled out of the parking lot, and then turned onto the street. The car accelerated with such grace, I felt as if I were in an airplane instead of a car. "I like this car!"

Tori laughed. "Yeah, so do I. It took me nearly five years to afford one."

We drove for what seemed like an hour, through back roads and winding hills. The scenery was beautiful with tall trees, green hillsides, and glimpses of San Francisco Bay. The Golden Gate Bridge lit up the dusky sky like a beacon among the gathering fog.

She asked how I managed to wander so far from home, and I explained my situation as if I were recounting a boring book report in a history class. I was hungry, tired, and low on hope of ever returning home. In truth, I was heading farther away. I didn't feel much like talking.

Tori pulled onto a long gravel road that ended at what looked to be a house built for Hansel and Grettle. The place was littered with colorful flowers, glittery colors, and so many wind chimes, they played like a New York symphony with the slighted breeze. Colorful flagstones marked the path to a large covered landing decked out in benches, fountains, and a small tea table for two. A large sign hung in the window, but I couldn't read it. When I returned home, the first thing I wanted to do was learn to read with my eyes.

I followed her into the building. Shelves were littered with nick knacks, fountains, sculptures, and dolls. Wind chimes were displayed in the windows, and animal noises came from the back. "You live here?"

She laughed. "No, this is my shop. I live in the back. I just need to check on the critters first."

I followed her through a maze of shelves, displays, and card stands. "Did you make all this stuff?"

She glanced over her shoulder. "Most of it. Some things are here on consignment."

I wasn't sure what that meant, but nodded anyway. She moved a few boxes and then jumped back. Two critters shrunk back into the shadows. She picked them up. "Hey you two, where have you been?" She looked at me and frowned. "Dave was telling the truth. How did you know?"

I shrugged. "When people lie, they emit an odor. He did not"

She lowered the odd-looking critters into a pen and checked the latch. "I accused him of stealing these little guys. They are very rare and worth over $500 a piece. Sold as a pair, they are worth much more."

I watched the fuzzy pair as they frantically licked the water bottle. "What are they?"

"Gold bar chinchillas. They have been missing for three days. Poor things are probably starving." She opened a canister and scooped out a portion of pellets. She spilled them into a dish in the chinchillas' pen. The pair scurried over to the food and eagerly feasted.

"Do you want to touch them?"

A surge of excitement and fear widened my eyes. "Uh, okay."

Tori reached into the pen and gently brushed the critters' back. "Just like this. Move slow and be gentle."

I reached into the pen and brushed the smaller animal. Her fur was so soft and dense, it felt like a combination of cotton and velvet. "They are very soft."

"Yes, they are. Chinchillas have the densest fur of any other animal. Unfortunately, people have killed these critters for their fur, nearly making them extinct."

I pulled my hand back and allowed the pair to finish their meal. "That's horrible and sad."

Tori secured the pen and double-checked the latch. "Yes, it is. Some of us are working on restoring their population. We are very careful about who we sell them to."

She finished feeding the rest of the critters before leading me out the back and into a small cabin. There were vines growing up the outer walls and a thick layer of moss on the roof. The bright red door was the color of candy, shiny and bright. Inside was a large living space, a tiny kitchen, and a short hall with three doors.

After showing me around, Tori started making us something to eat. I sat at the counter, sipping a glass of water.

Tori looked up from chopping broccoli. "So, you said people emit an odor when they lie. Care to explain?"

I explained how I was born blind and developed senses that provided me information about my surroundings and the people I encountered. "Everyone has a particular scent. That scent can be altered by certain emotions, foods, and synthetic perfumes. When people lie, they smell like strong vinegar because they are nervous."

She smiled. "Are all people nervous when they lie?"

I turned the water glass in my hand. "I think lying is hard for most people, but not all."

"You seemed pretty certain that Dave was telling the truth."

"He was telling the truth."

She nodded, but her face looked troubled. "I need to call him to apologize. He is a great worker."

After we had dinner, she called Dave.

"Thanks, Desmond. If it wasn't for you, I would've lost a loyal employee."

I smiled. "It was nothing, Tori. I did what I could. Actually, I wanna thank you for bringing me here. If not, I would've spent the night on that bench."

"Sure, honey," she answered.

Since there weren't any other rooms in the cabin, except for Tori's small room, she asked me to stay there. But, out of timidity, I chose to stay on the couch for the night. She provided me with pillows and a comforter.

"Get some rest, honey. Tomorrow, I'll drive you to Mill Valley." With that, Tori closed the lights leaving a small lamp beside the couch open.

I closed my eyes and saw a mirage of images in my mind. When I was blind, this was almost impossible. I thought I would just live a life, depending on my other senses... knowing people, attitude, and traits by touching, smelling, and feeling. I never thought that I'd be able to visualize it like this.

Suddenly a flash of lightning struck outside. It was followed by a booming thunder that chilled my nerves. In no time, rain came pouring down. I have always been scared of thunder but it was much scarier with lightning. Back then, I would refer to it as the wrath of the gods.

Unable to sleep, I raised my hand and drew it near the lamp. Shadows formed reflections on the ceiling. Pleasantly distracted from the raging storm, I continued to play, forming different shapes in the shadows. I saw this at a movie called, *The Greatest Showman*, and have been fascinated with hand shadows ever since. I formed a moose, a horse, a dog, and a graceful dove. Relaxed now, and feeling much calmer, I closed my tired eyes and fell asleep.

I awoke to the scent of fresh coffee and sizzling bacon. Tori was singing quietly, dancing and swaying to music I couldn't hear. When she saw me looking at her, she blushed and removed the buds from her ears. "You're awake."

I sat up and moved the covers aside. "Yeah," I said groggily.

"Would you like something to drink? Hot tea? Coffee? Cocoa?"

When I heard cocoa, my eyes lit up—a familiar and comforting treat. "Cocoa would be great, thanks!" I stood and started folding the blanket and comforter. I stacked them neatly on the couch and placed the pillow on top.

Tori smiled as I sat down at the counter. "Did your mother teach you to do that?" She gestured to the folded blankets.

"My sister and I were taught to clean up after ourselves."

She laughed. "Well, that's refreshing. Most kids I know have never folded a blanket in their lives." She stirred milk in a pan and added cocoa powder and honey. Then, she added a dash of red powder."

"What's that?"

She followed my focus on the pan. "Hot cocoa."

"No, the red stuff you added."

She laughed. "That is my secret ingredient. Cayenne pepper."

I wrinkled my nose. "Cayenne pepper? In cocoa?"

She finished stirring the concoction before pouring it into a mug. She took a bowl out of the refrigerator and scooped a huge puff of whipped cream on top. She sprinkled a bit of golden sugar on top before presenting it to me as if it were a golden chalice. "Try it before you turn your nose up."

I smelled the contents and brought it to my lips for a cautious sip. The rich, creamy chocolate was better than any cocoa I had ever tasted. I took a bigger sip and smiled. "This is so good! What makes the whipped cream taste sweet?"

"I add a bit of vanilla and coconut sugar while I whip it up. I like having it in my coffee."

I took another sip. "I can't even taste the pepper."

"I'm glad you like it." She pulled out fresh-baked biscuits from the oven, added them to our plates along with scrambled eggs and bacon. "Bon appétit."

I had no idea what that meant, but I was sure gonna enjoy this meal. She set a bowl of butter in front of me, along with some peanut butter, marmalade, and something black."

I watched as she smeared the black stuff onto her biscuit and eggs. It smelled sharp, like beef bullion only more condensed. "What is that?" I pointed to the jar of black spread.

She smiled and lifted the bottle with pride. "This is Marmite, a yeast extract. Would you like to try some?"

I shook my head, but my curiosity got the best of me. I dipped my finger into the tiny dollop she offered. It was very salty and had a tang that would taste good on steak, but there was no way I was going to ruin my eggs and biscuit with the stuff.

"Good?"

I wrinkled my nose. "It's okay."

She laughed. "It's an acquired taste. I grew up with it. My parents were British. They put Marmite on everything."

I shook my head in disbelief, and then added a generous portion of butter and marmalade to my biscuit. The first bite was heaven on my tongue. Long strings of sharp cheddar cheese stretched out. I immediately took another bite, and then another biscuit.

Tori's brow arched. "You like the biscuits?"

I nodded enthusiastically. "They have cheese in them. I've never seen biscuits with cheese. Where did you find them?"

"I made them the old fashioned way with butter, flour and buttermilk."

"My mom does that too, but she never added cheese. I'm gonna have to tell her about this."

After breakfast, I helped with the dishes and with opening Tori's shop. Dave called later to say he couldn't make it to work that day because his child was sick. Tori understood, but the look she gave me was forlorn.

"I'm sorry, Desmond. I cannot leave the shop unattended."

Part of me felt sad, but another part of me felt relieved. It was hard to explain, but I really enjoyed being here with Tori. "I can help, if you'd like."

Her face brightened. "That would be great. I'll even pay you."

"With more biscuits?"

She laughed. "Yes, and a bit of money. How does $8 per hour sound?"

I had never earned money for work—ever. "Perfect."

"Okay, let's start with feeding the animals and cleaning their pens. I also have a cow and two goats to milk."

My confidence shattered. "Uh, I've never milked anything, and I don't know much about the other stuff."

"Well, today is a good day to learn. Come on, we'll start with the milking."

I followed her out back where the cow and goats waited at the pasture gate. She grabbed a few halters and handed one to me. I looked at the thing that resembled a clump of knots. We entered the pasture and she slipped the large halter onto the cow's head. I watched as she tied the knot to secure the halter. She tied another one on one of the goat's heads.

"Okay, now you try," she said, gesturing to the smaller goat.

I slipped the halter over her tiny nose and flipped the long strap over her neck. I tied the knot, but Tori corrected it.

"Over the loop, or it will be hard to get loose."

I tried again and she nodded with approval. Leading the small goat, I followed her and the other two animals to a red barn that reminded me of candied apples. The cow entered a stall as if she knew exactly what to do. The goat did the same. I led my goat to the open stall as well. We closed the gate behind them all and allowed the lead ropes to drape to the ground.

Tori opened a tin container and scooped out some pellets. They smelled a bit like fresh-cut grass. She filled the cow's bin, and then the goat's. I got to feed the smaller goat.

"I like to give them a little something to keep them relaxed," Tori explained. She fetched three large buckets from a cabinet and handed one to me. "Place it under the goat, like this." She positioned the container under her goat, just in front of the hind legs. Following her lead, I did the same with my goat.

She pushed a stool toward me. "Have a seat." I did. She pointed her index finger down. "Now, grab my finger as if it were a pole, pinky side down." I did. "Good, now gently squeeze your index finger, and then your middle finger, ring finger, and pinky as if you are squeezing liquid from a tube." I did as she instructed. "Good. Now, while you do that, gently pull downward." I tried a few times until the motion became comfortable.

Holding the goat's tits felt very different from Tori's finger. The goat was ... squishier. I did the same motion with my hands, but very little milk came out.

"Squeeze a little harder, Desmond. You're doing great."

I did as she suggested and nearly jumped as a thick stream of milk hit the pail.

Tori laughed. "That's it! You did it. Now keep going, she's quite full." She took a seat beside me to milk the larger goat. When they were done, we both moved to the cow. Tori took two udders and I took the other two. The job went much quicker with both of us doing it.

I watched as Tori filtered the milk into glass containers and placed them into an ice bath that Tori had prepared before she started milking. We released the animals to the pasture and tossed them a few flakes of hay. A flake was a hand width wide, I was told, about four inches.

After washing our hands, we went back to the store. Tori left me to watch the counter while she went back to the house to prepare our lunch. She said that she'd cook some pasta which made me excited. I love pasta above all food. My favorite is Chicken Pesto. It is an Italian dish that Mom used to cook for us. I said, "used to" because after my operations, our diet switched to plain vegetables. Mom said that it was for my recovery and that it was good for my health.

Tori's lunch did not disappoint. It was fantastic, and the garlic bread proved worthy of a third helping. My stomach felt ready to burst. Tori slid the newspaper toward me. "Do you know these two?"

I looked at the words and reminded her that I had not had time to learn to read print. "What does it say?"

She pulled the newspaper back in front of her. "It looks like your parents are not the only ones looking for you. Do you know Netta and Joe Prescott?"

The blood in my face sank like lead in water at the mention of their names. "Uh, yeah, why?"

"They are looking for you as well. I'm going to close shop early today and drive you to the bus station where you can continue on home. Is that okay?" She folded the page and stuffed it into her bag. "I'll inform the police. They can call your parents to let them know you are safe and where to pick you up at the station."

"I know my way home from the bus terminal. I have walked that mile dozens of times."

"Still, I want to let them know where you will be."

As promised, Tori drove me to the bus station and waited for my bus to leave before returning to the shop. She had given me three $20 bills and told me to keep them in my pocket just in case. It was hard saying goodbye to her. I would have loved to help her more, but I missed my family and it was time to go home.

The bus groaned its way up the hill toward the bridge, but before it made it, smoke billowed from the engine and the bus jerked forward. The driver pulled over and announced that help was on the way. Everyone would be transferred to the next bus. It would be awhile, so many people got off and decided to wait outside. It sounded like a better idea than sitting in the smelly old bus, so I filed out with them.

I noticed a young boy sitting on the bridge with his bare feet hanging over the edge. He looked sad, so I made my way toward him. His pants were torn at the hems and his shirt was smudged with dirt and grime. He looked as if he'd been crying. I sat down beside him. "Hi, I'm Desmond." I extended my right hand toward him the way my dad did when he met strangers.

The boy took my hand. "Tom." He had short, curly black hair, and his skin was so dark, he looked as if he'd been dipped in dark chocolate.

"You look sad."

Tom wiped his face and sniffled. "I ran away from my foster home, and now I have no place to go. I'm hungry and tired."

"Why did you run away?"

He held up his arms. They were badly bruised. His lower lip was swollen. "My foster father has a temper and I seem to make him angry a lot. He hurt me this time, so I ran away."

"Wanna come with me?" I gestured to the broken down bus and the passengers. "They're sending another bus soon. I can buy your fare."

His dirt-smudged face brightened. "Yeah, I would."

We walked over to the bus together, but the bus driver looked at Tom and shook his head. "Sorry, son. You can't ride the bus without shoes. Besides, you need exact change to purchase a fare. I cannot take a twenty spot."

Tom shuffled his dirty bare feet and looked down at the ground. "That's okay. You don't have to stay with me. I'll be alright."

"I'm not gonna just leave you. We'll find another way."

There was a small town just across the bridge. "Hey, are you hungry?"

Tom nodded enthusiastically.

I pointed to the golden arches that stood out on the horizon like two angelic clouds. "Let's get something to eat."

We walked together across the bridge, talking about our adventures and the people we had met. Tom told me about making a raft out of a pallet and how he had almost drowned while trying to paddle it across the bay. A fisherman picked him up and took him back to shore. That is how he ended up here. He told me about a stray dog that bit him. Holding up his right arm, he pointed to where the small dog had broken the skin.

We stopped at the middle of the bridge to enjoy the magnificent view of the bay. Boats meandered by, gliding slowly over the water as if defying time. The cars on the Golden Gate Bridge looked to be as small as the Matchbook cars I used to play with as a young child.

Tom stood at the railing with one foot perched on the lower rung. "So, where are your parents? Why are you traveling alone?"

Emotions flowed within me like the water below. I thought of my family and how worried they must be. I wished there was a way I could tell them that I'm okay. "I was chasing a balloon and got lost. Two older people tried to keep me, so I ran away. I've been trying to get back home ever since. I have been away from my family for days."

Tom looked out at the water. "They must miss you, yeah?"

I nodded. "I suppose. I've never been separated from them before. After my operation, they became very protective."

His gaze snapped back to me. "You had an operation? Are you sick?" He looked me up and down as if looking for clues.

"No, not sick. I was born blind. My doctor gave me new eyes so that I could see, but my first operation was unsuccessful. So, I had another operation."

Tom scrunched up his nose. "Being blind sounds scary."

"Not really. Before I had vision, the world seemed much smaller. It never extended beyond what I could touch, hear, taste, or feel. Now that I can see, I know that it is much larger than I had ever imagined. After all the adventures I've had these past days, I've realized that I was not just blinded by lack of vision, I was also ignorant."

Together we watched as the sun sank slowly behind the hills; its reflection on the bay resembling fire.

Tom's eyes lit up. "Hey, you wanna see something cool?"

I shrugged. "Okay."

"Come on."

I followed him off the bridge and across a wide lawn. At the center, there were two buildings made of bright orange brick and a lot of windows. I remembered seeing something like them on television. "Where are we?"

Tom placed his finger to his lips. "Shh, be quiet." He crouched low, waving for me to follow.

Vines climbed up the back of one building. I watched in amazement as he carefully pulled them apart to reveal a narrow door. It squeaked as he opened it. I followed him through a long, dark tunnel that made me feel claustrophobic. After what seemed to be a ridiculously long stretch, the darkness opened to a magical room filled with waxy-looking figures of Walt Disney, Mickey Mouse, and other Disney characters. "I know this place."

Tom beamed a smile and spread out his hands like a circus master. "Welcome to the Disney Family Museum."

I looked around at the colors that seem to glow in the darkness. "I've seen this place on television once, but it is even more magnificent in person."

"I figured with your new eyes, you might like to see something magical."

I touched the life-sized figures and marveled at the happiness they invoked in me. "How did you know about the small door?"

"I knew the gardener here. I used to help him clean the place and he gave me food. He told me about the door and said it would offer shelter when the weather was bad. It kind of became my sanctuary when my foster parents turned mean. I could be gone for days and they never seemed to notice or care."

My heart ached a bit at the thought of not having anyone to care for me. "That must be hard." I chuffed. "My family cares for me a bit too much, I think. They rarely let me out of their sight."

Tom gave me a tour of the museum, offering a bit of history along the way. We passed a theater but the door was locked. My eyes widened as I spotted a huge, life-sized train.

Tom followed my amazement. "You like trains?"

"I do! When I was younger, my Aunt Corazon and Uncle Ed gave me a train set. I loved how it sounded as it rolled over the tracks. The rhythm of its motion often put me to sleep. I played with that train every day." I touched the massive engine that seemed to glow. The paint and chrome were so shiny, I could see my reflection. "I want to be an engineer when I grow up."

"Me too," said Tom, but there was a sadness in his eyes. We moved on to another room.

A huge orb seemed to float near the ceiling and I wondered what kept it up. I reached up to touch it, but couldn't quite reach.

Tom pointed to the magical orb. "During the day when the museum is open, that ball glows like a big neon meteor. It even changes color."

"How does it stay up?"

We heard footsteps approaching and Tom grabbed my arm. We ducked behind a huge table with curtains hanging down. The footsteps grew louder, echoing off the walls like my racing heart. Black, shiny boots entered the room and hesitated. Tom pressed his finger to his lips, silently telling me to stay quiet.

The man turned around shining his flashlight upon every wall and corner. I scooted my foot back. Seemingly satisfied that all was well and good, the man turned around and left the room. Tom tapped my shoulder and gestured that I follow him back to the tunnel. I breathed deep not realizing that I had been holding my breath. We ran through the tunnel and scampered out the door like two mice who had just gotten away with a bounty of cheese.

In what seemed to be half the time it took us to find the museum, we reached the bridge. Both of our stomachs growled. "Hey, are you hungry?"

Tom's eyes lit up. "I'm always hungry."

I gestured across the bridge at the familiar golden arches. "I have a bit of money. How about we get ourselves something to eat?"

Tom's pace quickened.

We made it to McDonald's but Tom was not allowed to enter the place without shoes. I told him to sit at one of the outdoor tables and I would get some food. Not knowing what he wanted, I bought cheese burgers, chicken nuggets, chocolate shakes, and fries.

His dark eyes widened when he saw the loaded down tray of food I carried toward the table. "Wow!" He reached for one of the shakes, stuffed the straw in with little care, and took a long draw of the creamy stuff. "This is good."

I started unwrapping a burger and took a bite. I handed him a burger and slid the tray of nuggets toward the center of the table. It was a true feast for two young boys, but we made quick work of it.

"Desmond?" Hearing that familiar voice caused the food to stick in my throat. I pushed it down with a sip of my shake and slowly turned around. Joe was standing right behind me. My heart felt ready to pound out of my chest.

Joe waved Netta over. "My god, boy, we have been worried sick about you."

Netta gave me a lingering hug. "Oh, sweet boy. Thank God you are all right."

Tom watched the exchange with casual interest. He was stuffing the last chicken nugget into his mouth as if it would walk away if he didn't eat it fast enough.

I gestured to him. "This is Tom."

Joe and Netta greeted my new friend, and then turned back to me. Joe nudged my arm. "Did you find your parents?"

I didn't trust this man anymore. If I told him the truth, would he take me with him again? It was a chance I was not willing to take. I took a sip of my shake and gave Tom a look, hoping he would understand. "Uh, yeah. They're coming back to get us any time now."

The way Joe looked at me and Tom made me shiver. Lying was not one of my super powers. "Come with us. Let's take you to Mill Valley."

My shake suddenly felt like mud in my mouth. I pushed it away. "No need."

Joe took a seat beside me on the bench. "No, I insist."

Joe grabbed my wrist and Netta held Tom.

"Let me go, Joe!" I shouted as I felt his grip tighten. He wrapped me in his arms and covered my mouth with his other hand. Tom fell unconscious as Netta put a handkerchief on his nose.

"You think I'll just let you go, Desmond?" He put me down inside the car.

"Let me go!" I pushed him hard which made him lose his balance. I broke away as fast as I could. Cold sweat covered my body.

"Hey! Come back here!" Joe started running after me.

"Wake up, Desmond!" the soft voice of my mom echoed in my ears. I felt delirious. I had to be.

Suddenly, I stumbled upon a rock that I had failed to notice, and everything turned black.

"Wake up! " the voices in my mind echoed. I wanted to open my eyes, but couldn't. My leg ached, the pain in my knee was excruciating.

Joe caught up with me and started shaking my shoulders. "No one messes with me, young man." I stumbled to my feet. The deafening sound of an approaching car startled me, followed by a blinding light.

"Wake up, Desmond." The voice sounded like it was miles away, yet still, I couldn't open my eyes no matter how hard I tried. The voice of Joe faded away.

A gentle hand nudged my arm. "Desmond, come on. Open your eyes, son."

I willed my eyelids to open, then squinted as bright light flooded my vision. "Dad?"

I heard my mother cry. My father held my hand. "Yes, son, it's me. Wake up, now, you're going to be just fine."

I heard the lights turn off and the voices of other people as they entered the room. One of them had a deep voice. My father released my hand. "Open your eyes, Desmond."

I tried again, forcing my lids to open. It felt as if sand were in my eyes, making it hard to keep them open. I could not focus on anything and the scent of alcohol and disinfectant assaulted my nose. A small lamp was lit at the side table. There were books stacked upon it. I recognized their covers. Mom had described the pictures on the front of each of them: *Huckleberry Finn*, *The Hitchhiker From Talue*, *The Magnificent Redwoods*, and *Tori Anderson*. They were familiar stories among my favorites.

"Mom?" I uttered as tears started to stream down my face. "J-Joe… He's trying to hurt me…" I said hysterically. My mom frowned.

"Who's Joe? Nobody's trying to hurt you honey." she said.

She lifted my head and drew my face close to her chest. "It's alright, honey. It's just a bad dream. Wake up now, Desmond." She kissed my forehead.

www.ingramcontent.com/pod-product-compliance
Lightning Source LLC
LaVergne TN
LVHW041549070526
838199LV00046B/1886